the CRiTTeR club

Amy the Puppy Whisperer

by Callie Barkley ♥ illustrated by Tracy Bishop

LITTLE SIMON

New York London Toronto Sydney New Delhi

LITTLE SIMON

An imprint of Simon & Schuster Children's Publishing Division · 1230 Avenue of the Americas, New York, New York 10020 · First Little Simon hardcover edition September 2020. Copyright © 2020 by Simon & Schuster, Inc. All rights reserved, including the right of reproduction in whole or in part in any form.

LITTLE SIMON is a registered trademark of Simon & Schuster, Inc., and associated colophon is a trademark of Simon & Schuster, Inc. For information about special discounts for bulk purchases, please contact Simon & Schuster Special Sales at 1-866-506-1949 or business@simonandschuster.com.

The Simon & Schuster Speakers Bureau can bring authors to your live event. For more information or to book an event contact the Simon & Schuster Speakers Bureau at 1-866-248-3049 or visit our website at www.simonspeakers.com.

Designed by Brittany Naundorff. The text of this book was set in ITC Stone Informal Std.

Manufactured in the United States of America 0720 FFG. 10 9 8 7 6 5 4 3 2 1

Cataloging-in-Publication data for this title is available from the Library of Congress.

ISBN 978-1-5344-6622-7 (hc)

ISBN 978-1-5344-6621-0 (pbk)

ISBN 978-1-5344-6623-4 (eBook)

Table of Contents

Chapter 1

Meet Marley

Amy twirled in an office chair as she read her book.

She was at her mom's veterinary clinic, which was next door to their house. Gail, the vet assistant, did not work on Sundays. So Amy was helping out by greeting her mom's patients.

So far, Dr. Purvis had seen

1

a hamster with a cold. She had checked out a gecko with a poor appetite. And she had prescribed ear drops for a bunny's ear infection.

Now Dr. Purvis was in the exam room with a cat who wouldn't stop scratching.

The waiting area was empty. Amy had time for another chapter of her book. She spun as she read.

She flipped pages as she rolled. She pressed on the lever under the seat. The chair dropped to its lowest setting.

Amy's eyes scanned the lines of text. Something big was about to happen with the dog main character.

Yip! Yip-yip!

Amy looked up from her book.
That barking. It was real. And
close by!

Yip! There it was again! It was
coming from the other side of the
front desk. But Amy couldn't see
over it. The office chair was still on
its lowest setting.

Amy stood up.

The woman who was standing there jumped in surprise. "Ah!"

That made Amy jump too. "Ah!"

"Sorry, I didn't see you there!" the woman said with a laugh. "Hello, I'm Tara. This is Marley."

Tara gestured down at the floor. "She's here for a few shots."

Amy peered over the desk. At the end of a red leash was a tiny beagle puppy.

Yip-yip! Marley looked up at Amy and wagged her tail.

Amy checked the appointment book. Marley's name was written in the time slot right after the scratchy cat.

"My mom should be out in a few minutes," Amy said. Then she peeked down at Marley again. "She's so cute! Can I say hello?"

"Of course," the woman said. "Marley is very friendly."

Just then the woman's cell phone rang. She looked down at the screen and sighed.

"Oh, I have to take this call," she said to Amy. "Would you mind holding on to Marley while I step outside?"

Amy beamed. "I'd be happy to!" she exclaimed.

Tara handed the leash to Amy. Then she hurried outside to answer her phone.

Amy knelt down next to Marley.
The puppy was up on her hind legs,
sniffing the front desk.

"What do you smell?" Amy asked her. She followed Marley's gaze to a jar on top of the desk. It was filled with Fitter Critter healthy dog treats. "Aha," Amy said. "You want a treat?"

Marley's tail wagged a little faster. Amy opened the jar and took out one treat. She closed her hand around it. Then she knelt down next to Marley again. Amy let the puppy sniff her closed hand. But she didn't open it . . . yet.

Amy had an idea.

"Sit?" Amy said to Marley. "Do you know how to sit?"

New Puppy, New Tricks

Marley stayed standing. She licked at Amy's hand and barked. *Yip! Yip!*

"Sit," Amy said again.

But Marley just kept trying to get at the treat.

Amy pushed down gently on Marley's behind. "Si-i-i-it," Amy said slowly as she did that.

Suddenly Marley got the

message. She tucked her hind legs
underneath her body and sat.

"Good girl!" Amy said
enthusiastically. She broke the treat
into two pieces. She gave one half to
Marley, who gobbled it down. Then
Marley stood up again. She licked
at Amy's hand.

"You want more?" Amy said.

"Can you sit first? Sit, Marley. Sit!"

Marley looked at Amy. She cocked her head to one side. Then Marley sat.

"You did it!" Amy cried. She rubbed Marley behind the ears. Then she opened her hand.

Marley took the rest of the treat. "Good job, Marley!"

"Wow!" came a voice from the door. Amy looked up. Tara was watching from the entryway. She had come back in time to see Marley sit. "You taught her to sit! Just like that?"

Amy handed the leash back to Tara. "Marley is a fast learner!" she said.

Tara reached down to pet Marley. But she was still looking at Amy in wonder. "Well, I think *you* must also be a very good teacher!"

The next day after school, Amy met up with her friends at The Critter Club. It was the animal rescue shelter the girls ran in Ms. Marge Sullivan's big barn.

Amy, Liz, Ellie, and Marion were pet sitting a dog named Bella and a kitten named Zoot. Their family was packing up to move into a new house, so the animals were staying at The Critter Club for the week.

"I've never seen a cat and dog get along so well," said Marion.

The girls were standing around Bella's dog bed. Bella was napping. Zoot had nestled into the fur on the dog's back. He was using Bella's big

floppy ear as a pillow.

"They're so cute together!" Ellie squealed.

Liz agreed. "Bella is so gentle," she said. "Even though she's twice Zoot's size."

Amy agreed. "It's like she thinks Zoot is her puppy." That reminded her of Marley. Amy told her friends about the adorable puppy she'd met at the clinic. "I taught her how to sit!" she exclaimed.

Ellie gave Amy a pat on the back. "You've always been good with dogs," Ellie told her.

"Me?" Amy replied in surprise. "I don't even have a dog." And her cat, Millie, was glad about that.

"I know," Ellie said. "But dogs love you. I think our dog, Sam, likes *you* better than *me*."

Marion smiled. "I'm good with horses," she said. "Not so much with dogs."

"And remember how Rufus loved you right from the start?" Liz pointed out.

Rufus was Ms. Sullivan's dog. When Amy first met him, Rufus had licked her all over her face.

Amy considered this. Were her friends right? *Did* she have a special connection with dogs?

What's Gotten into That Dog?

On Tuesday, Amy checked out a stack of books from the library.

After dinner, she curled up with the biggest one: *Your New Best Friend.* Amy knew a few things about training dogs. But she thought she could learn more. What kinds of tricks could she teach Bella? And how?

Amy skimmed the table of contents.

Just then the doorbell rang. "I'll get it!" Amy called to her mom.

She opened the front door.

There on the front porch was Tara, holding Marley in her arms. Tara looked very upset.

"I'm so sorry," Tara said, "but is your mom here? Marley swallowed something. I'm not sure what. And I don't know what to do!"

Marley barked cheerily at Amy.
Yip-yip! She looked happy as could
be. But Tara's worried expression
made Amy's heart race.

"Come in," Amy told Tara.

Then Amy hurried to get her

mom. Dr. Purvis grabbed her vet bag. The three of them sat down in the living room.

Tara put Marley in her lap. Dr. Purvis sat next to them. Marley let Dr. Purvis hold her mouth open and shine a light inside.

said at last, "Marley seems fine." The puppy was busily sniffing between the sofa cushions. "But it would be wise to get an X-ray." Dr. Purvis stood up. "Let me make a phone call."

Dr. Purvis went into the kitchen. Amy waited with Tara and Marley. Tara looked less nervous now.

"I'm still getting used to Marley's quirks," Tara said with a sigh. "She sniffs everything. And she also wants to *taste* everything—even things that are bad for her. But she doesn't like it when I take them

away. She even nipped at me a couple of times!" Tara looked down at Marley and frowned. "Didn't you, Marley?"

Amy picked up *Your New Best Friend*. She flipped it open to a chapter she'd seen earlier called "Nip? Nope!" "Maybe there's some good advice in here," Amy said hopefully.

"I can use all the help I can get!" Tara exclaimed.

So Amy read one of the tips out loud.

Make a loud "Ouch!" when a puppy nips during playtime. It will let the puppy know "That hurt!" Then ignore the puppy for a few minutes. Over time, the puppy will learn that if she nips, playtime is over.

"That makes sense," Amy said. "Puppies sometimes nip each other when they play." Amy had noticed exactly that when they'd had a litter of puppies at The Critter Club.

"Marley just needs to learn that it's not okay to nip during playtime with *people*," Amy added.

Tara read the book over Amy's shoulder. "This is *so* helpful," Tara said.

Just then Dr. Purvis came back in.

"I called the animal hospital," she said. "They can see you tonight, since we can't open the clinic right now."

Tara thanked Amy and Dr. Purvis so much and told them she'd keep them posted.

Amy was glad her mom thought Marley would be fine, but she did wonder *what* Marley had swallowed!

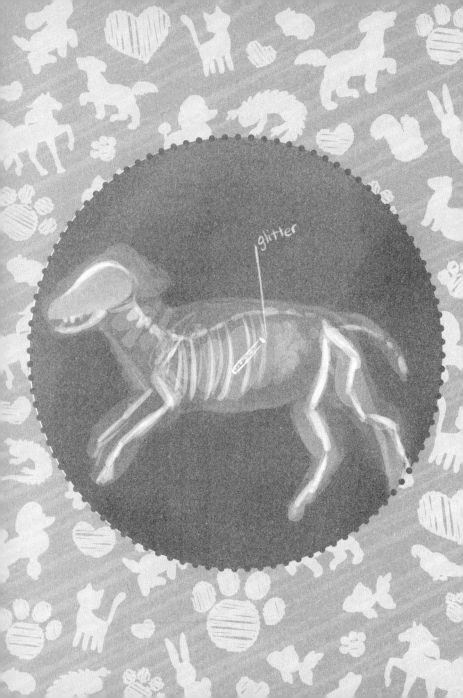

Chapter 4

Amy Gets a Job

Amy couldn't stop giggling. "I can't believe it," she said.

Her mom was tucking her into bed. They'd just gotten a call from Tara. The X-ray had shown that there was a small tube in Marley's stomach. Tara had recognized the shape. It was a tube of glitter from her crafting table!

"It will pass out of Marley in a day or two," Dr. Purvis said. "You know, when she does her business."

"I know!" Amy said between giggles. She tried to catch her breath.

"And won't it be . . . sparkly?"

That made Dr. Purvis giggle too.

She reached to turn off Amy's lamp.

"Hey, Mom, what do you think of Tara's idea?" Amy asked.

On the phone, Tara had asked Amy if she did puppy training— and if she would want to train Marley!

"I mean, she knows I'm not really a trainer, right?" Amy added.

Dr. Purvis smiled and nodded reassuringly. "Yes, but she can see you have an interest in puppy training. And a talent for it."

Amy grinned. "It *does* sound like fun," she said.

"It's totally up to you," Amy's mom told her. "Why don't you think about it and we can let Tara know tomorrow."

"Okay," Amy agreed.

Dr. Purvis kissed Amy and then flicked off the light.

Amy drifted off to sleep with a smile on her face.

The next day, Amy was on Critter Club duty with Ellie. They met up inside Ms. Sullivan's barn. Zoot was doing figure-eights around Bella's legs while Bella drank from her water bowl.

Amy cleaned Zoot's litter box. Meanwhile, Ellie tidied up Bella's sleeping crate. While they worked, Amy told Ellie about training Marley. After some thought, she'd called Tara and told her she would take the job. It was also a major plus that Tara owned a bookstore.

Because she had offered to pay
Amy . . . in books!

"Wow!" Ellie exclaimed. "Amy, you'll do great."

"Thanks," Amy replied. "Saturday's our first session." That reminded her: Amy was scheduled to be at The Critter Club

on Saturday. "Oh! Ellie, could we switch our Critter Club days? Could you sub for me on Saturday, and I'll take your day next Tuesday?"

Ellie nodded. "No problem," she said. "In the meantime, I guess we can enjoy taking care of a dog who already knows all the tricks."

Amy laughed. Ellie meant Bella, who definitely didn't need training.

Sit.

Stay.

Heel.

Leave it.

51

First Day of Puppy School

Amy rang the doorbell at Tara's house.

Immediately, she and her mom heard a *yip-yip-yip* from inside. It grew louder and closer. There was a soft thud on the other side of the door. It was followed by frenzied scratching.

Amy and her mom smiled at

each other. It was Marley!

"Okay, down, Marley," Tara said, opening the door. She held Marley by her leash. "Hello!" Tara cried out over Marley's loud barking.

Tara waved them inside.

"What a lovely home," Dr. Purvis said.

Amy looked around. No wonder Tara didn't want Marley chewing on everything. Her house was filled with nice things. Her sofa and armchairs were white and spotless.

There were beautiful pillows all around. The fireplace mantel held expensive-looking art objects.

Suddenly, Tara spotted Marley sniffing at a particularly shaggy pillow. Amy had to admit, the pillow did look pretty appealing to a puppy.

"No, Marley!" Tara called. She grabbed the pillow before the puppy could.

Amy looked down at Marley. "I have an idea," Amy said. "There's a cue called 'leave it.' That way, you can tell Marley to leave things alone that she shouldn't chew on. I think that's the one we'll work on today."

Amy explained that she'd work with Marley by herself first, and then bring Tara in.

Tara nodded. "Sounds like a dream." She held out the leash for Amy to take. "Good luck!"

Tara and Dr. Purvis stayed inside to chat while Amy led Marley into the backyard.

Tara's backyard was fenced in on all sides. *Perfect*, thought Amy. It meant Marley could be off leash.

Amy detached the leash from Marley's collar.

Immediately, Marley started sniffing at Amy's pockets.

Amy laughed. "Can you smell them already? You do have a good nose!"

One pocket was filled with Fitter Critter healthy dog treats. Amy knew Marley liked those.

Her other pocket was filled with Puppy Snax. Amy had heard they were like candy for dogs: *super* tasty. Amy bet Marley would like those even more.

Amy had a plan for teaching Marley "leave it." She had read all about it in *Your New Best Friend*.

Step one: Allow the puppy to sniff a treat in your closed hand. She may paw and lick and try to get at it. Do not let her have it. Wait for the puppy to get bored or turn away.

Step two: Praise the puppy and give her—SURPRISE!—an even tastier treat from your other hand hidden behind your back.

Repeat steps one and two again and again. Every time the puppy looks or pulls away from the closed hand, say "leave it." Then reward her with the tastier treat from the other hand.

Amy began with step one.

She reached into her right pocket. She wrapped her hand completely around a Fitter Critter treat. Then she held her closed fist out to Marley.

Marley sniffed it. Then she began to lick Amy's fist. She nudged at the hand with her nose. She barked at it. She licked it some more.

Amy expected that. She waited patiently for Marley to get bored or look away.

And she waited.

But Marley kept on going— nosing and licking and barking. She wanted that treat!

Amy's hand was dripping with doggie drool. And Marley's licking really, really tickled.

Amy didn't open her hand. She *couldn't* open her hand. Marley needed to learn.

But Amy started to wonder: *Was Marley going to learn?*

Chapter 6

Good Reviews
Travel Fast

"So how did it go?" Ellie asked Amy at school on Monday. "You had your first training session with Marley!"

The girls had just sat down at the lunch table.

"Yeah," said Liz. "Ellie told us about your new job!"

"Is Marley a good student?" Marion asked.

Amy sighed. "Well . . ."

Ellie laughed. "So that's a no."

Amy told them that she'd tried to teach Marley to leave it. "We worked on it for a whole hour," Amy said. "Marley would not give up. She really wanted that treat. At last she

got distracted by a bird. When she looked away, I could reward her."

Liz clapped. "That sounds like a start!"

Amy frowned. "I don't know. I *think* she's getting it. I'm going back next weekend. Thanks again for being my sub, Ellie."

"No problem," Ellie replied. "Liz and I had fun with Bella and Zoot."

"Zoot got stuck behind the cupboard," Liz added. "So Bella crawled under to help her out."

"Awww," Amy said. "That's so sweet!"

After school, Amy sat down to do her homework. But she had trouble concentrating. Right next to her was the big bag of books Tara had given her on Saturday. Tara hadn't been sure what Amy liked to read, so she had brought Amy lots of different kinds of books.

Amy peeked inside the bag. Such beautiful, crisp, brand-new-smelling books!

Amy glimpsed the word "mystery" on one of the covers. She was pulling it out when she heard the phone ring.

"Amy, it's for you!" her mom called from the other room.

Dr. Purvis brought over the phone. As she handed it to Amy, she whispered, "It's a friend of Tara's."

"Hello?" Amy said into the phone.

"Hi, Amy," said a cheerful woman's voice. She introduced herself as Cynthia. "I know Tara from the dog park. Today she was telling me how great you are with Marley!"

Amy felt flattered. "Thank you," she replied. "But we've only had one lesson."

"Here's the thing," Cynthia continued. "I have a new puppy too. He's ten weeks old.

A boxer named Louie. And I was just wondering, do you have time for another puppy on your training schedule?"

"Oh!" Amy said. She was caught by surprise. She didn't exactly have a "training schedule."

Amy didn't know what to say. The silence on the phone line was making her nervous. Cynthia was waiting.

"Okay!" Amy blurted out. "Sure!"

Amy scheduled a time with Cynthia. Then they said good-bye.

Her mom raised her eyebrows curiously. "Did you *want* to say yes?" Dr. Purvis asked.

Amy thought about it. "I'm not totally sure," she said honestly. "But I want to give it a try."

Who's Walking Who?

Amy had agreed to meet Louie on Tuesday. But that meant she had to switch her Critter Club day again. This time, Marion had offered to swap.

Louie jumped up on Amy as soon as she and her mom got there.

"Down, Louie," Cynthia said.

But Louie didn't listen. Amy knelt

down to pet him so he wouldn't
need to jump up to say hello.

"Louie has a lot of energy,"
Cynthia said apologetically.

Dr. Purvis nodded. "That's pretty normal for a puppy," she said. "He'll probably get calmer with age."

Cynthia sighed. "I do walk him a lot. He needs to get his energy out. But he's always pulling at the leash. It's like Louie is taking *me* for a walk!"

It was clear Louie needed to learn to heel. Luckily, Amy had read that chapter in *Your New Best Friend*.

So Amy took Louie, his leash, and a pocketful of Louie's favorite treats. They went for a walk.

It was a very slow walk.

Every time Louie pulled at the leash, Amy stopped walking. Or Amy would *try* to stop. Sometimes Louie kept pulling, and Amy got pulled along.

"Whoooooaaaa!" Amy cried. "Whoa, Louie. Stop!"

Eventually, Amy got Louie under control. She would stand still until he stopped pulling. Then Amy would give him a treat. "Good boy, Louie," she said.

They'd walk a few more steps.
Louie would start pulling again.

By the time Amy and her mom got home, Amy was exhausted.

"My whole body is sore," she said. She flopped into a kitchen chair. Dr. Purvis started a pot of water for pasta. Then she checked the phone messages.

There were two. And they were both for Amy—one from a neighbor, one from the town librarian.

Both about puppy training.

"Two more customers!" Dr. Purvis said.

Amy slumped in her chair and closed her eyes. This was a good thing . . . right?

Amy the Puppy Whisperer?

That night, Amy stayed up late reading dog training books. She felt as if she was studying for a test.

Amy read all about teaching a "quiet" cue. The neighbor who'd called, Mr. West, had a puppy who barked a lot. Amy told him she could come to meet his puppy the next day.

Amy also studied up on how

to teach "come" and "stay." The librarian, Mr. Spencer, had a puppy who wanted to chase cars. "One time he ran out into the street!" Mr. Spencer said.

Amy read and read—page after page. Her eyes grew heavy. She rubbed them and tried hard to stay awake. She had not planned to take on so many puppies. But this felt important. Like these puppies—and their people—needed her!

At school on Wednesday, Amy felt her mind wandering during math. Mrs. Siena asked them to write a word problem.

Amy started writing.

Marley eats three treats. If she gets five more, will she finally learn to leave it? Oops. Amy erased that last part.

At quiet reading time, Amy read the dog training book she had brought to school. When it was time for recess, Amy was still in the middle of a chapter. So she brought the book out to the playground.

Amy told her friends about the two new puppies.

"Whoa," said Liz. "That makes four, right?"

"Do you have time for that many?" Marion asked.

Amy bit her lip. She did feel stressed. But she *wanted* to be able to do it. "I can handle it," she said.

After school, Amy spent all afternoon on puppy training.

She went down the block to meet Mr. West's puppy.

She scheduled a lesson with Mr. Spencer's puppy.

She and her mom searched online for the best-tasting dog treats.

After all that, Amy was up late again—doing her homework.

By Thursday, Amy was dragging through the school day. But as she walked home, she realized something.

She didn't have any puppy training that afternoon. It was the first time all week!

Amy dropped her backpack in the front hall of her house. She took off her shoes. She skipped her after-school snack.

Instead Amy went upstairs. She flopped onto her bed. And she did something she never did. Not unless she was sick.

Amy took a nap.

Her head sank heavily into her poofy pillow.

And then suddenly, Amy's mom was gently shaking her awake. It felt like only ten seconds had passed. But Amy's clock showed otherwise. She'd been asleep for two whole hours.

Her mom was holding the phone.

"Honey," Dr. Purvis said, "Liz called. Did you forget to go to The Critter Club today?"

Today? Amy thought groggily. But today was . . .

Amy sat up in bed, suddenly wide awake. "Thursday!" she moaned. "Oh no! I completely forgot!"

A Tough Choice

Amy took the phone from her mom. "Liz, I'm so, so, so sorry," she said. She was practically in tears she felt so bad.

But Liz was really understanding. "Don't worry," she told Amy. "I know you've been super busy with the puppies. I only called to make sure you were okay."

But Amy still felt terrible. She had missed so many days at The Critter Club! These puppy lessons were getting to be too much.

Amy felt she had to make it up to her friends.

She was hosting their weekly Friday sleepover, which was . . . tomorrow! Amy decided she'd make it up to them then.

So the next night, Amy ordered pizza. It was Ellie's favorite.

Amy got out a deck of cards for Liz's favorite game—Go Fish.

And Amy pulled out two of the

books from Tara. They were from a new horse series. She knew Marion would love them.

When her friends arrived, Amy welcomed them.

"I've got a lot planned," Amy
told them. "But before any of that,
I have something to say." Her voice
quivered a little bit. Tears welled up
in Amy's eyes.

Liz, Ellie, and Marion huddled
around her. "What's the matter,

Amy?" Liz asked gently.

Amy took a deep breath. "I'm so sorry I've been neglecting The Critter Club," she told them. "And I want to let you guys know, I'm going to stop doing the puppy training."

"Oh!" Ellie cried. "But you love puppies!"

"And you're so good at it!" Liz added.

Amy sniffed. "I'm too busy. I can't do both—puppy training *and* The Critter Club," Amy said. "I have to choose one. And I choose The Critter Club."

Marion was quiet. She was tapping her chin slowly.

"Wait," Marion said. "What if . . . you *didn't* have to choose?"

Amy looked confused. "What?"

Marion's eyes twinkled. "What about puppy training . . . *at* The Critter Club?"

Amy stared. Her jaw dropped open. She looked at Liz. Liz looked at Ellie.

Ellie squealed.

"Marion!" cried Liz. "You are a genius."

"Nah," Marion said humbly. "Well, an organizing genius, maybe." She laughed.

"It solves everything," Amy said. "I won't miss my days at The Critter Club. I'll ask the owners to bring the puppies *there*."

"And we can help!" Ellie said. Then she shrugged. "If you want," she added.

Amy jumped up and down. "Yes! It's perfect! It's the perfect solution!"

Chapter 10

The Critter Club to the Rescue!

Amy smiled as she walked into the barn. It felt good to be back at The Critter Club!

All four girls were there. It was Saturday, so it was Amy and Liz's day. But Marion and Ellie wanted to be there too. It was the first ever puppy training class at The Critter Club!

Tara had dropped off Marley for her second lesson.

Bella and Zoot were very interested in the puppy. They came over to sniff Marley and say hello.

Marley started jumping excitedly. Zoot got nervous and hid behind Bella. Bella was perfectly calm, as always. She was as gentle with Marley as she was with Zoot.

"Okay, Marley," Amy said. She led Marley away by the leash. "Let's get to work."

Amy decided to start easy by practicing how to sit. Would Marley remember? Amy held out a treat in her closed hand. "Sit," she said.

Marley did not sit.

But way across the barn, Bella sat. She was following Amy's cue.

Amy laughed. "Good girl, Bella!"

And then Amy had an idea.

"Bella, come!" Amy called out.

Bella trotted over and stopped at Amy's feet. Amy gave Bella a treat and some pats.

"Bella, sit!" Amy said. Bella sat. Amy gave her another treat.

Meanwhile, Marley was watching it all.

Then Amy turned to Marley. Once again she held out a treat. "Sit, Marley," Amy said.

Marley glanced at Bella, sitting by her side. Marley looked up at the treat.

And then Marley sat! "Yes!" Amy cried. "Good Marley!" Amy gave her the treat.

Liz, Ellie, and Marion had seen it too. They clapped and cheered.

"All right, now let's show Marley how to do 'leave it,'" Amy said to Bella. And with that, Critter Club puppy training was officially in session!